MW00912281

Mollie's Miracle

Renée Holmes Kent

New Hope
Birmingham, Alabama

New Hope
P. O. Box 12065
Birmingham, AL 35202-2065

Dewey Decimal Classification: JF
Subject Headings: PREJUDICES—FICTION

Scripture quotations identified CEV are from Contemporary
English Version. Copyright © American Bible Society 1991. Used
by permission.

Cover design by Cathy Lollar

ISBN: 1-56309-207-7

N977105•0597•5M1

Happy twelfth birthday
with love
to my horse-loving girl in action
Mary-Alison Kent

And to our friends, who were the inspiration for
Yoshi, Caitlyn, Savanna, Beth, Detrick,
and Rose & Jess Potter

To all children
of all sizes and shapes, handicaps, colors,
economic standing, and nationalities—
Jesus made you special order. He looks on your
heart; He loves what He sees!

"God is love. If we keep on loving others, we will
stay one in our hearts with God, and he will stay
one with us" (1 John 4:16 CEV).

1

Midnight Madness

For the second night in a row, Mollie Jane McCalla couldn't sleep. She had tossed and turned so much that her sheets and blanket looked like a pile of wadded laundry.

With a heavy sigh, she sat up in bed. Her tongue ran over her teeth, all bumpy with braces. She was tired of her teeth being in jail. She was tired of being 11 years old. She was tired of lying in bed when there was so much going on in her life!

There were so many reasons why she couldn't sleep that she wasn't sure which one was keeping her awake the most. Since she was wide awake, she decided to list the possibilities.

For one thing, the second school semester

of the middle school in Mountain Lake, Tennessee, would officially end in 16 more hours. Miss Plerkins had told her sixth-grade class to wear old clothes, because there would be a special activity on this last day of school. Mollie had been wondering what it might be.

Still, that wasn't the main reason Mollie was wide-eyed at midnight. Sure, she couldn't wait to run out of that dusty, stuffy school building and take her last ride on the old yellow school bus. It wasn't that the bus was so bad—it was the rotten boys who rode with her. They were loud and obnoxious. The worst of them all was Detrick Silver, the biggest football player on the seventh-grade team. He had tormented her and her friends for the whole semester. Just thinking about him made Mollie shudder. She decided to turn her thoughts to happier things—like summer freedom with her best friends, Caitlyn, Savanna, and Beth.

Her friends. . . *hmm*. Maybe they were the reasons Mollie couldn't get some shut-eye. They had all been close since kindergarten, except for Savanna, who had moved in midway through the first grade. But lately, Mollie noticed that Beth and Savanna didn't seem to

2

be getting along as they once did. Their friendly teasing now had hints of unkindness.

Mollie liked her friends so much, but they just did not seem to be fitting together comfortably these days. It troubled her to think of anything happening to their special friendships.

Of course, they all were getting into that age where playing with dolls and their favorite childhood games were definitely out. Each girl was developing her own interests.

For instance, Savanna was a petite gymnast and future cheerleader for the seventh-grade football team. While almost everyone in the sixth grade had braces or would be getting them soon, Savanna had perfect, sparkling white teeth that looked great against her milk chocolate complexion.

Savanna, the shopping mall maniac, wore the cutest clothes of all the girls in Mountain Lake. But after all, Savanna's dad owned a manufacturing business and could afford to give his only daughter the best gifts money could buy. So Mollie was happy for her friend.

Mollie secretly longed to be half as beautiful and feminine as Savanna, who had moved here five years ago with her parents, Antonio and Christiana Linstead, from Montego Bay on the tropical island of Jamaica. She had the coolest accent and most beautiful black braids, always beaded to match her brightly colored designer clothes.

Then there was brainy, practical Beth, short for Elizabeth Bernardine Scofield. She owned maybe a total of three pairs of summer shorts and tops that stayed stuffed in her drawers, until Beth pulled them out and rewore the crumpled fabric several times between washings.

An honor student who had never in her life made an A without a plus sign behind it, Beth was far more interested in reading books and caring for her family's farm animals. She didn't have time to think about anything else that might interfere with preparing for her future career as a medical doctor or large animal veterinarian.

The funny thing about Beth was that she never cared whether her hair got messy or her socks matched. And she always had a walkman hooked to her otherwise empty belt loop. While everyone else listened to the latest music, Beth chose nonfiction audio books, preferably written on the adult reading level. These books were too boring and technical for Mollie, but after all, she was sure that Beth's brain had hers beaten by a mile in the race for smarts. But Beth wasn't snobby or braggy about it in the least.

It was just Beth's parents' style to encourage using the good brains God had given each of their children. Her Dad was a college dean of medical science at a Nashville university, and her mom was a computer whiz for a major corporation. Beth's three sisters and two brothers were all super brains, too, but Beth was also funny, without even meaning to be. To Mollie, that was what made Beth such a special friend to be with.

And finally, her all-heart friend, Caitlyn. Mollie smiled to think of her freckle-faced, green-eyed buddy, a loyal pal through thick and thin. Just give her a ball and bat and a hot dog with chili only from Yummy Freeze Drive-Thru, and she was a happy camper.

Growing up with three older brothers had rubbed off on Caitlyn Marie Armstrong. What a tomboy! Maybe it was because her dad called her "Chipper" and taught her how to play football before her second birthday.

Not many people knew how beautiful Caitlyn was becoming behind the playground grime. She had the most awesome sunlight blonde hair that often got crammed underneath a baseball cap or gathered into a streaming ponytail that nearly reached her waistline.

Maybe what made her pretty was that Caitlyn was so unaware of it herself. But the whole Armstrong family, even all those brothers, thought Caitlyn was tops.

Mollie could tell that Caitlyn got her great sense of humor from her mom Terri. She had been Mollie's volunteer nurse's aide when she had to have her tonsils removed a few years ago. Caitlyn's mom could cheer up a sour pickle, and so could her daughter. But somehow Caitlyn seemed a little quieter these days, and Mollie wondered why.

Mollie loved each one of her friends with all her heart. But she wished they could get along better with each other. *Something is pulling us apart*, Mollie thought, *and I guess it's up to me to be the glue for our group.*

It might take a miracle, but she hoped

that this summer, the funny foursome would grow closer than they had ever been before. She prayed for each of her special friends and that their sleepover at Rose Potter's farm would be a happy launch into a carefree summer.

2

Mollie's Dream

After her talk with God, Mollie tried to go to sleep, but it just wasn't working. She still hadn't figured out what was *really* keeping her awake!

She sat up in bed and counted the days until her birthday. In exactly five days she would be 12 years old. Mollie sighed. That still wasn't why she couldn't catch some Z's, though birthdays were just about the greatest things since horses . . .

Oh, horses! Yep, that's why I can't sleep, she thought. A dreamy smile crept across her face in the semi-darkness.

She gazed at her orange guppies in the bubbling tank at the foot of her bed. The plush green water plants swaying in the aquarium became a grassy paddock filled with mares and foals and yearlings and stallions and . . . .

Bleep, bleep, bleep, bleep, bleep. . .

"Mollie," came a familiar voice from a far-away horse barn. "You're sleeping through your alarm again! Time to get ready for your last day of school. Just look at your bed-covers. Have you been riding horses in your sleep again?"

Mollie opened one eye. Her mother was turning off the blaring alarm clock beside the bed. "Oh, I guess I did get to sleep after all. Mom, can I go to Rose's after school?"

"I don't know," said Mom, slightly amused. "*Can* you?"

Mollie sighed. Whenever she said "can I" instead of "may I," Mom always turned into some sort of grammar professor or something. Even at an important time like this! But Mollie went along with it.

"Mom, *may* I go to Rose's after school? Red needs a good brushing, and she's due to foal any day now!"

Rose was not only one of Mom's best friends, but she was also Mollie and Savanna's choir director at church. She and her husband,

Jess, raised and showed Tennessee walking horses all over the eastern United States.

In fact, Rose and Jess Potter owned last year's World Grand Champion, and they were teaching Mollie everything they knew about the horse business. It was no wonder that Jess and Rose Potter had become Mollie's favorite adults of all time.

"Land sakes, haven't you visited Cedar Hills Farm three times already since Saturday?" Mother asked, looking doubtful. "Besides, you and your friends are going to spend tomorrow night in the barn. Don't make a nuisance of yourself, Mollie Jane."

Mollie sighed. When Mom used her middle name, she meant business. This was not a good sign. But what did she mean by "nuisance"? Didn't Mom know by now that Jess and Rose were like her very own grandparents? Why wouldn't they love to see Mollie anytime she could come?

"But Mom," she began, trying to make her case without being disrespectful, "Rose needs the help, with the rest of the new foals coming soon. I'll do all my home chores this morning before school," she said, trying to smile through her early morning wake-up fog.

"*Hmm*, I suppose you can go, but only for an hour or so. Now try to hurry, or you'll miss the bus for school." Mom leaned over and kissed her forehead. Mollie didn't mind a kiss now and then, so long as it wasn't done in public.

"Thanks, Mom. You're the greatest."

"Yeah, right, kiddo," Mom chided, tousling Mollie's light brown curls. Mollie scampered ahead of Mom across the hall to grab a quick bath ahead of her older sister, Charity, who took the longest showers known to the human race.

Mollie was suddenly charged with energy to get through those boring chores as fast as possible. She'd rather clean stalls at Cedar Hills Farm any day than fold her clothes and empty dumb old waste baskets that were always full.

But doing those chores was a small price to pay to get to breathe hay and leather and horses for an hour. Someday, she would get to breathe that wonderful horse smell nonstop, when her greatest prayer would be answered.

Mollie's dream? To own a horse of her very own. She prayed constantly with all her heart, believing that some day the time would

11

be right. So far, God was letting her get to know horses through her friendship with Rose. For now, she was trying to be thankful and patient, still hoping for that special someday when . . .

But why torture herself with such glorious thoughts? She knew in her heart that it would take a miracle to convince Mom and Dad to let her have a horse. That was a big expense. And they were already making payments on three sets of braces—for Mollie, Charity, and her big brother, Eric.

Since Eric would be a senior this fall, there would be college expenses on top of the regular bills. Mollie figured a horse was the last thing Dad would consider at a time like this. Even if she saved her meager allowance, it would take about 20 years to save enough!

Still, she was sure that somehow, someday her horse prayer would be answered. As she whisked through her chores, she whispered, "But, dear Lord, please don't make me wait too long."

3

Anybody Got a Glue Gun?

Later, at school, Miss Plerkins returned the final term papers of the semester. Then she ushered Mollie's class into the gym for a special end-of-the-year activity, along with all the other sixth-grade classes.

Mollie scanned the crowd for Beth, Savanna, and Caitlyn. Soon, as usual, they were huddled together, talking about Mollie's favorite subject.

"Oh, for the last time, do we have to talk about horses *again?*" Savanna fumed. "My brain is fried after our final exams. Besides, it's too hot in here to talk about anything. Give it a rest, Mollie. Don't you ever think about anything besides those ornery animals?"

"As a matter of fact, I do," Mollie sniffed.

"Like what, for instance?" challenged Savanna, tossing her long, jet-black braids.

Mollie paused, twirling the tiny natural curls that had escaped her ponytail. Come to think of it, Mollie struggled to find any other subject that was worth talking about. *"Well ... ,"* she began, stalling.

"That's a deep subject," said Caitlyn, her green eyes dancing. "I'm often amazed at how deep wells can be. See Savanna? Mollie can talk about wells."

Mollie smiled like a good sport as her friends doubled in laughter at her expense. Finally, Beth rescued her.

"Stop teasing her, you guys. She can't help it if she likes horses. As a matter of fact, I know how wonderful it is to appreciate the beauty of a well-trained, carefully groomed horse."

Caitlyn giggled. "You're talking like a horse encyclopedia."

"Why thank you," Mollie said with a grin. She and Beth exchanged a high five, while Caitlyn and Savanna rolled their eyes hopelessly.

A piercing shrill from the gym's old sound system interrupted their discussion. Miss Plerkins jumped away from the microphone as if it might bite her. Then she uncertainly eased her way back toward the mouthpiece as Mr. Atkins, the principal, adjusted the sound controls.

"As you all know," she began, "we've been studying the subject of prejudice in social studies class throughout the spring term. Would someone volunteer to share the meaning of the word, 'prejudice'?"

Everyone looked at each other and groaned. Miss Plerkins frowned, scanning the audience. "I was hoping for a little more enthusiasm. Beth Scofield, would you please come to the microphone and define 'prejudice' for us?"

Mollie reached out to touch Beth's shoulder as she made her way down the bleachers. "Go for it. You can do it, Beth."

"Brown-noser," teased an unidentified onlooker.

"Teacher's pet," muttered someone else.

"Boring," Savanna mumbled, propping her head in her hands. The bright gold and purple beads in her hair clicked against each other. A long, whiny sigh filtering through the crowd signaled that the students agreed with her.

"Come on, Savanna!" coaxed Mollie, "Beth needs our support." But Savanna just blankly stared at the ceiling.

Beth cleared her throat and quoted the definition perfectly. "Prejudice—an unfair judgment or opinion formed without examination of all the facts; hatred or suspicion of a particular group, race or religion. Prejudice often causes detriment or injury to a person or group because of these ignorant and unfair judgments."

"Very good! Thank you, Beth," said Miss Plerkins. "We will end our study of prejudice today with a variety of exercises."

"She's not going to make us do jumping jacks and sit-ups, is she?" whispered Beth, as she took her seat in the bleachers again.

Mollie giggled. She knew Beth absolutely detested gymnastics and physical education.

"Not those kinds of exercises," said Savanna, a bit annoyed.

Caitlyn scolded them. "Cut it out, you guys. Let's just get through the day without a fuss."

Mollie sighed and began to say, "I wish . . ." then she stopped. Despite her prayers to be the glue that held together her best friends, Mollie sensed a big summer mess brewing. What she really needed to be was super glue!

4

The Great Wall of Prejudice

At first no one was excited about the day's activities. Pretty soon the opinion changed. For the rest of the day, class was held outside under the enormous oak trees in front of the school building.

Mr. Morehouse took a group of students through a number of challenges that persons with disabilities face. Some students wore blindfolds and had to grope through tasks, such as taking a report to the school office.

Others, including Mollie, were confined to a wheelchair. She couldn't believe how hard it was to maneuver a wheelchair across the parking lot and into the school to get books out of her locker. Her upper arm muscles burned from wheeling herself over uneven pavement and gravel and sticks outside and bumpy door facings inside.

Meanwhile, some of the students were actually assigned to ignore or tease those on crutches and in wheelchairs or who could only use one arm throughout the day.

How humiliating! This exercise certainly isn't promoting peace, Mollie thought. *How can our teachers go along with this?*

Miss Plerkins painted the students' faces. Some students had flowers on their foreheads, and other students had animals painted on their cheeks. These two groups of students were to pretend that they didn't like or trust each other.

The trouble was that Savanna, Beth, and Caitlyn were "flowers," while Mollie was an "animal." When it was time for lunch, the "animal" group wasn't allowed to eat with the "flowers."

Instead of picnicking under the trees with the "flowers," the "animals" had to sit in the hall in front of their lockers and not speak as they ate lunch. Mollie felt incredibly left out.

By the end of the day, the sixth grade was

divided into a number of little groups that were supposed to dislike each other. Boys against girls, "flowers" against "animals," students with fall birthdays against students with spring birthdays. Left-handed students snubbed right-handed students. Students with eyeglasses ignored students without glasses. Even students who had pets disliked those who had no pets.

Mollie had never seen so many people pitted against each other in her life. And at school! She couldn't believe nice, orderly Miss Plerkins would go for this kind of activity.

Then Mollie started to get the message as she noticed that the other students looked pretty miserable, too. She began to understand why it was so terrible for people to judge others by the color of their skin or by their religions or by some silly marking on their faces.

But that wasn't all the sixth-graders were doing. For every prejudice represented, the teachers had students add a large cardboard "brick" to a Great Wall of Prejudice that grew and grew throughout the day across the school parking lot. By sixth period, Mollie couldn't see over the wall. Even Coach Wilson, the tallest teacher in school, had to stand on a step ladder to get the last few bricks in place. The school buses couldn't even get into the parking area and had to line up along the street instead.

By the time Mollie was starting to get nervous, the best part happened. Coach Wilson blew his whistle. Then all the students helped knock down the wall of prejudice. Cardboard "bricks" went flying everywhere as all the students joined in tearing down the wall.

At last, "animals" and "flowers" grinned at each other. All the students came together for a big group hug in the middle of the schoolyard, and Principal Atkins took their picture.

Miss Plerkins tried to yell over the pandemonium. "Our study on prejudice has *ended*, but I hope that you will *begin* your summer ready to fight the effects of prejudice in our society and our world."

Everybody yelled and whooped and cheered to the tops of their lungs.

Mollie had to admit to herself that she now understood more about how prejudice creates trouble for people, but one question just wouldn't stop running through her mind: *What can a sixth-grader like me do about such a gigantic problem?* It was too hard to think about. After all, she was just Mollie, and her big job was to be the glue for the funny foursome. And that alone was going to take a miracle.

5

Of Mice & Mollie

The bell sounded. Mollie, Savanna, Caitlyn, and Beth rubbed the paint off their faces. Everyone scrambled to the buses.

"Wow, I'm glad that's over," said Caitlyn, slinging her gym bag over her shoulder.

"Me too!" yelled Savanna, doing six cartwheels in a row. "School's out for summer!"

"Speaking of which," said Mollie, "are you guys still going to Rose's tomorrow night for our end-of-school party?"

"I can't wait!" said Beth, as they chose their seats on the bus. "Are we really going to sleep in the barn, Mollie?"

"That's the plan," she answered proudly since she had helped arrange the sleepover.

"Goodie! I'll bring the chocolate candy," said Caitlyn, who loved chocolate best next to softball.

Savanna's mouth puckered as though she had just eaten a lemon. "Will the barn be clean? I mean, horses are pretty, but I don't want to *smell* like one."

Beth giggled. "Just watch where you step, Savanna. You don't want to get those designer sneakers dirty."

"*Yeuuewww*," said Savanna, squeezing her eyes tight with an all-over shiver. "I don't see why we have to sleep in the barn." Everyone giggled.

"Don't worry, Miss America," said Mollie, "I'll bring an extra blanket to spread out just for you. There's nothing to worry about."

"Except mice," said Caitlyn, her mischievous emerald eyes watching for Savanna's reaction.

"Caitlyn, don't!" warned Mollie, but it was too late.

Savanna was already shrieking with disgust. "Mice! You're kidding, aren't you?"

"Be reasonable," said Beth with authority. "Barns with a few mice are perfectly normal. A mouse isn't even remotely interested in hurting you."

Savanna looked faint. "I don't think I'd better come after all. Mom's been promising to take me to the mall."

Mollie poked Savanna's arm. "Don't worry. Mittye Kitty is Rose's favorite cat. She takes care of most of the mice in the barn. You've got to come! It's our big chance to actually spend the night all together. And you know how great Rose is. It'll be fun!"

"Please, please, come," the girls all pleaded with Savanna—except Beth, who remained quiet.

After a long while, Savanna agreed. "OK, but if I even so much as see the tip of the tail of one single mouse, I'm out of there."

Just as the problem was solved, someone thumped Mollie hard on the head. It was seventh-grade football player Detrick Silver. Leaning across two seats, he asked. "Hey, did someone say something about mice?"

Then he held up a whole cage full of mice right in front of Savanna's slightly turned-up nose. "I'm adopting these over the summer. They're from the science room."

Savanna gasped and buried her face in Mollie's shoulder. But Beth turned and stared down Detrick with a withering look. "That's a lot of responsibility, Detrick, looking after the lab mice like that. Are you sure you're up to the challenge?"

"You girls think you're so smart," Detrick said, mocking them. "I'll show you who's up to challenges." Then he looked at Mollie. "Just watch out, if you know what's good for you," he added with a scowl.

He clambered off the bus at the long drive to his house in the woods. The girls gazed after him.

"What did he mean by that?" Caitlyn wondered aloud.

"Oh he's just *prejudiced*—against girls, that's all," said Beth, giggling. "Nothing to worry about."

But Mollie wasn't so sure. Her hazel eyes followed Detrick as he disappeared into a thicket of trees that seemed to swallow up the small house. She hadn't trusted Detrick ever since he had sneaked down the road into Rose's pasture one early evening in the spring. He had thrown mud at the grazing horses, including

Mollie's favorite, Red! Fortunately, Jess caught him in the act and made Detrick help give the horses a good brushing and wash the fence where the mud had splattered.

Yes, Mollie would definitely have to keep her eyes open for trouble. But she decided not to worry too much. After all, summer vacation had arrived, and Detrick Silver was not going to spoil it!

6

Mollie's New Friend

Mollie's stress from the long day melted in the late afternoon sun that streamed through the tall, sweet-smelling cedar trees and into the windows of the Potters' barn. Dawdling, she wandered beside each stall, greeting the horses one by one.

Then she went into the tack room and began clearing a table for refreshments for tomorrow night's party. Her spirits were lifting already.

"Mol——lie!" it was Rose's soprano voice calling. She came through the open end of the barn and into the tack room. "I have a new friend for you to meet."

An Asian boy a little older and taller than

Mollie followed Rose. His dark eyes twinkled pleasantly, and his jet black hair caught the slight breeze blowing through the barn.

"Yoshi Kugimoto, this is Mollie. Mollie, Yoshi is here from Tokyo, Japan. He is staying with Jess and me for 10 whole weeks," Rose began, her contagious smile widening. "He's 14 years old, and he never came close to a horse in his life until he arrived here this morning. Won't we have fun?"

Mollie was startled, but immediately liked Yoshi's dancing eyes and toothy smile. She liked his manners, too. She wished boys from America were nice enough to bow like Yoshi was doing. It made her feel special.

"It is happy to meet you," said Yoshi, reaching out to shake Mollie's hand.

Mollie smiled, glancing at Rose, who gave her a wink. Then she replied, "I'm happy to meet you, too, Yoshi. You speak English already?"

Yoshi looked at Rose. His confused expression made his face look like a big question mark.

She explained for him. "In Japan, the schools teach English. Yoshi knows some

29

English, but we must help him. OK, Mollie? I'll be counting on you this summer."

"Great!" said Mollie with a big smile. "This will be fun."

Rose handed each of them a grooming brush, and the two followed her to Red's stall. As they gave Red the best brushing of her life, she told Mollie how Yoshi came to be with them quite unexpectedly.

"A friend of mine directs a program for foreign exchange students. Yoshi was assigned to a family in west Tennessee. They had an emergency at the last minute and could no longer host his visit. So my friend called me and asked if Jess and I would take care of Yoshi during his stay in America."

"Wow," said Mollie, smiling at Yoshi. "Don't worry, Yoshi. You're going to have a great time this summer. Do you like horses?"

"Hoss?" asked Yoshi, pointing to Red. Then he smiled grandly. "Like hoss very much!"

Mollie grinned. "We're going to get along just fine," she announced.

While Mollie busied herself feeding the animals, Yoshi disappeared into the house and returned with a small bundle wrapped in white paper with pink flowers on it.

"For Mollie," he said, handing her the package.

Mollie loved surprises and nearly tripped over a wheelbarrow accepting his gift. "A gift? I can't believe it," said Mollie to Rose.

Rose laughed. "Yoshi came to America with a whole suitcase full of gifts from his homeland for the people he meets during his stay. It looks like Christmas inside the house. He brought a whole boxload for Jess and me."

Mollie's fingers were soiled from handling hay and grain. So she swiped her hands on her jeans and carefully opened the papers. Inside was a delicate, handpainted porcelain bell on a loop.

"Wow! I'll hang it in my bedroom. Thank you!" she exclaimed.

Yoshi bowed politely. So Mollie bowed, too, and their heads clunked together. Yoshi and Mollie laughed as they held their heads.

It didn't matter one bit that Yoshi could not speak much English at all and that Mollie could not speak Japanese at all. The two communicated quite well. They groomed and fed the horses together, getting along with a little sign language.

Soon, Yoshi had taught Mollie to say, *Konichiwa* (Kon-ee-chee-wah), which means "Good afternoon" in Japanese. Mollie taught Yoshi to say, "What's up, buddy?" just for fun. Then she introduced him to hot cinnamon candy, which she almost always carried in her pocket.

Yoshi tasted the candy and fanned his mouth. "Oh, no! Goodbye, my family!"

"Oops," Mollie said to Rose. "I shouldn't have given him something so hot. Are you OK, Yoshi?"

But Yoshi was smiling from ear to ear. "More candy, please."

"OK," said Mollie, handing him several more candies. "He likes it, Rose!"

Rose stuck her head out of a stall to see Yoshi pop another fireball into his mouth and tease about the "fire" on his tongue. "You two are going to be great friends. I can see that already."

Mollie nodded. "And I can't wait for Caitlyn, Beth, and Savanna to meet Yoshi, too!"

"Yes," said Rose, "and maybe you can introduce him to Detrick Silver. You know, he lives right down the road from here."

Mollie stared at Rose in disbelief. "You're kidding, right? After that overstuffed football player threw mud at your horses? Detrick Silver is the last person I would introduce Yoshi to."

Rose walked toward Mollie and hugged her. "Now Mollie, are you going to hold that against Detrick from now on?"

"I just don't trust him, that's all," said Mollie. "And why should I trust him? I bet he's never done anything nice in his whole life. We need to protect Yoshi from meeting Detrick. Why, if he meets someone like Detrick he might go back to Japan thinking all Americans are real jerks."

Something in Rose's blue-gray eyes twinkled and saddened at the same time. "Now Mollie, can you be honest? Why don't you tell me how you really feel? Have you forgotten how to forgive?"

"No," said Mollie, not quite sure how to end such an uncomfortable conversation. "I can't help how I feel."

"Is that so?" Rose smiled. Then a sly look

flitted across her face. "We'll see about that. Remember that God loves Detrick too."

Mollie felt her face grow warm. She liked Rose and wanted her approval. So she decided not to say what she was secretly thinking: God can't possibly love someone so mean and smelly and low-down and stubborn and sneaky as Detrick Silver! Can He?

7

Dried Squid & Other Surprises

Mollie made sure she was the first to arrive at Rose and Jess's farm Thursday night. She wanted to help introduce Yoshi to each of her friends.

Rose had outfitted Yoshi in western riding wear. He was even sporting a wide-brimmed straw hat and boots. But that wasn't the only surprise.

The picnic table underneath the shade of a large maple tree was decorated with crepe paper streamers and balloons. In the center of the table was a cake that read, "Mollie's Almost 12—Happy Birthday!" Savanna arrived, taking lots of pictures with her new camera.

Jess was grilling hamburgers and hot dogs

in his "Butter Up the Cook" apron. Rose and Jess seemed to know how to make every occasion special.

Caitlyn arrived with her baseball mitt, bat, and ball. So, as the other girls arrived, a baseball team grew, with Rose as the coach. To Caitlyn's delight, Yoshi was a good hitter and a great catcher.

Beth called meeting Yoshi an "educational opportunity." That meant she was glad Yoshi had come to stay for the summer. She seemed to like looking through the photo album Yoshi had brought from Japan.

The album contained photos of his family, his father's restaurant business, and his school. There were also lots of colorful postcards of sites in Tokyo, including the bullet train and the downtown city lights at night.

A pocket at the back of the album held Japanese coins shaped like a donut, with a red ribbon tied to each one. With a polite bow Yoshi gave a coin to each of his new friends.

Savanna whispered to Mollie, "I remember what it felt like coming here from Jamaica when I was seven. I'll try to help Yoshi feel at home."

Mollie was beginning to feel more confident that this summer would be the finest ever. That is, until Yoshi decided to share a favorite Japanese snack food with the girls—dried squid. Caitlyn was the only one who could swallow it down, but the tears in her eyes indicated her misery.

Mollie, Beth, and Savanna spit out their squid in a birthday napkin and Mollie slipped it into the trash without Yoshi noticing. Rose and Jess just laughed.

"I have a snack for Yoshi to try," said Caitlyn, wiping the tears from her eyes. She pulled out a two-pound box of homemade chocolate candies. All the girls rushed to take a generous helping, if only to get the fishy squid taste out of their mouths. Rose didn't even object to candy before supper. In fact, she had a big piece of peanut butter fudge!

Yoshi tried chocolate for the first time. He crunched into a nutty candy. Suddenly his mouth puckered and his eyes watered. "Too sweet!" he declared. The girls took an extra handful each of the chocolate candy and munched away.

"We're glad Yoshi doesn't like it. All the

more for us," said Caitlyn, tossing her ponytail with a giggle.

Then Yoshi took out his package of dried squid. "Mmm, better taste," he said, as the others broke into fresh laughter.

"Frankly, I prefer a good old-fashioned hamburger off the grill," said Jess, sinking his teeth into a steaming, juicy burger with all the trimmings.

After their dinner, Yoshi brought out another snack, but this time it was minty Japanese gum. Mollie liked it because it never lost its flavor, and she chewed on the same stick for the rest of the evening.

Mollie helped Rose and Jess saddle a couple of horses, and they all took turns riding around the barn. It was by far the best party Mollie could ever remember . . . until Detrick Silver showed up with his dad.

Mr. Silver was doing some field work for Jess. Mollie couldn't believe that Detrick was going to "help." While Mr. Silver talked with Jess, Detrick approached the girls.

He gestured at Yoshi, who was riding Hershey, the calmest horse in America. "Hey, who's that . . . ? He dropped his voice, but

Mollie knew he called Yoshi by a descriptive name he didn't want Rose to hear.

Mollie felt fire rise up to her ears. Detrick was not going to pick on Yoshi because she wouldn't allow it.

Rose took Detrick to meet Yoshi. Though Detrick avoided making eye contact, at least he was civil. "Yoshi's a pretty good baseball player, Detrick," said Rose. "Maybe you guys can get together over the summer."

Detrick mumbled in response, drawing lines in the barn's dirt floor with his foot. Eventually, he wandered out of the barn.

As soon as he was out of hearing range, the girls huddled. Mollie let her steam out. "He makes me so mad! Why is Rose so nice to Detrick? He's up to no good."

"Did you see the look on his face?" asked Savanna. "He was poking fun at Yoshi without even saying anything. I know!"

"He would have said plenty if Rose hadn't been standing nearby," added Beth.

"Son," called Mr. Silver, "we need to get going. We have an early day tomorrow."

"Uh, just a minute, Dad." Detrick's voice came into the barn. "I'll meet you at the truck."

While Jess walked Mr. Silver to the driveway, Rose encouraged the girls to be patient with Detrick. "God loves Detrick, too, and so must we."

As the Silvers' truck pulled out of the long winding driveway, Mollie noticed several white somethings scurry across the barn in different directions. Horses began to whinny and kick up against the sides of their stalls.

Squeak!

Mice!

Yoshi hopped off Hershey, who was nervously pawing at the ground. Before anyone could speak, Savanna was standing on a chair in the tack room next to a wall phone. She was calling her Mom to come get her.

Beth caught and examined one of the little creatures. "Why, these are the lab mice from school. Detrick was supposed to take care of them for the summer. This one is Alex, and he's scared to death."

"Not as scared as I am," shivered Savanna.

"Let's catch them all before Mittye Kitty gets to them," said Caitlyn, who wasn't afraid to touch mice or frogs or anything like that.

Just then, Red groaned from her stall. Checking on her, Rose announced, "She's showing signs of delivering a foal soon. It could be tonight!"

This time it was Mollie who squeaked. "Goodie!" she said. "But Rose, what will we do about these mice?"

Rose thought a minute and directed her down to the old storage supply shed for an unused aquarium. Mollie found it and dusted it off with her shirttail and dashed back toward the barn.

Savanna was already waiting for her mother by the picnic table, her overnight bag in hand. "Thanks for a very mice time—I mean a very nice time," she said with a shaky laugh.

Mollie smiled and sighed. "Savanna, we'll miss you tonight. Won't you stay? We've caught almost all the mice."

"No, Mollie, I just don't belong on a farm. The hay makes me sneeze, and animals are dirty, and smelly and, well, I hope you understand."

Mollie waved goodbye and walked a little slower toward the barn. This had been a great day, but with his little surprise Detrick had really fouled up her plans big time. Now with Savanna scared off, the gang couldn't settle their differences as Mollie had hoped.

She gazed at the twilight sky and saw the first star of the evening. Everything looked so peaceful up there, so right.

Caitlyn called out, "Mollie, where's that aquarium? Hurry!"

"Coming!" Mollie yelled back, and she walked quickly into the barn. She would deal with Detrick's little prank later. Right now, there was a mouse hunt, a party, and a birth going on in the barn, and she didn't have time for Detrick Silver!

8

Mollie's Magic

Between catching 12 tiny science lab mice, putting down fresh straw in Red's stall, and cleaning up after the party, the girls were exhausted. Rose looked around the barn with a sigh of tired satisfaction.

"Mollie, come up to the house to get us if Red needs attention during the night," she said, tweaking Mollie's freckled nose. Mollie felt proud to have the trust of Rose and Jess with the care of Red, their favorite brood mare and pleasure riding horse.

"Oh, Rose, what if Red should have her foal tonight?" Mollie's excitement oozed out all over.

Rose gave Jess a knowing look. "Let's just

wait and see. You girls try and get some rest, OK? If Red needs you, you'll hear her. Come along, Yoshi."

"*O-yasumi nasa i*," said Yoshi, politely bowing to the girls. Then he added, "Good night."

As the girls watched through the window, Yoshi, Jess, and Rose walked under a glowing full moon across the yard and into the comfortable old farm house. Mollie sighed. "Don't you wish American boys were as polite as Yoshi is?" Beth and Caitlyn giggled.

The girls spread out their sleeping bags over the concrete floor of the tack room. "This is cool, Mollie! I wish we could do this every night," Caitlyn said, yawning. She took down her ponytail and brushed her cornsilk mane.

Beth checked the mice to make sure they couldn't escape from their new home in Rose's aquarium. She dropped a handful of grain into a jar lid and filled a cup of water for the mice to feast on overnight. "I feel like a veterinarian already," said Beth. "I hope that Red will cooperate and foal tonight."

One by one, they snuggled into their sleeping bags and tried to keep their conversation going long into the night. Falling into a troubled sleep, Mollie dreamt of hundreds of mice running loose in the barn and scaring the horses. She chased mice—and Detrick Silver—before she fell into a deep sleep.

When Mollie awakened, the sun's first rays were streaming into the barn. Rose's cheerful voice drifted through the barn and clued her in that the most important event of the year had occurred during the night.

Oh, why didn't I wake up? Mollie asked herself as she arose carefully and tiptoed around her slumbering friends. She joined Rose and Yoshi, who was still sleepy and rubbing his eyes, in Red's stall.

Lying in the straw next to Red was an absolutely beautiful red foal. She was the image of her mother, except for a perfect, tiny gray heart that marked her little pink nose. Her fluff of a mane stood straight up like a miniature Mohawk hair cut. Her bright brown eyes seemed to soak in all the details of her surroundings. Red seemed as proud of her baby as any human mother.

"What will you name her?" cried Mollie, tingling with excitement.

Rose smiled mysteriously. "As soon as I saw her, I knew this foal had your fiery spirit and friendly personality, Mollie. Her barn name will be Mollie's Magic."

Mollie was speechless. She threw her arms around Rose and hugged her tightly.

Then she ran to summon Beth and Caitlyn. Together, the girls dashed back so as not to miss anything. Yoshi stared at the mother and baby in amazement and tried to say something in English, but it came out in Japanese.

Rose smiled broadly. "I think Yoshi is trying to say that baby horses are the best things since dried squid."

The girls shuddered and chorused, "Yeeuuw!"

9

How Do You Love a Bully?
(Very Carefully)

For an hour, they watched the foal struggle to find a use for her wobbly legs. Finally, Mollie's Magic was on her feet. Soon she discovered what Rose called "the groceries"—her mother's warm, sweet milk. Watching silently, Mollie fell in love with her little namesake.

Just then, Detrick and his father drove up to begin their day of work in the field on Jess Potter's tractor. Mr. Silver strode into the barn. "Well, well, I see you've had a busy night," he said, chuckling. "Son, come see the newcomer."

With his mug of morning coffee, Jess followed Detrick into the barn. "So how's Detrick this morning?"

"Fine, thanks, Sir," said Detrick. It burned Mollie up how Detrick could act like a perfect saint to adults, and be a complete jerk in reality. It just wasn't fair!

"Come see Mollie's Magic," Jess said, turning to greet Mr. Silver. While the adults walked over toward the tractor at the other end of the barn, Detrick peered into Red's stall for a look at the foal.

Mollie frowned at Detrick, but he avoided making eye contact with the girls. "Big deal," he mumbled, shrugging his shoulders. "I've seen hundreds of horses. This one's nothing special. Kind of scrawny, if you ask me."

"We didn't ask you, you big bully," said Caitlyn, with her hands on hips.

This was about all Mollie could take. She and Beth glanced over at the container of mice. "You forgot something last night," Mollie said firmly.

"You sure did," said Caitlyn, crossing her arms in disgust.

Beth was composed and matter-of-fact. "I'm sure the science teachers will be interested to know about the traumatic lives of their lab mice over the summer break," she said.

"Who cares?" said Detrick, shrugging. "Besides, I figured that foreign kid could use a little excitement. If he can't handle it, let him go back where he came from."

"That does it," Mollie hissed. She felt her face grow hot, and she tried to keep her voice from shaking with anger. But it wasn't working. "First you pick on us, then you infest the barn with a bunch of mice."

"Mice? What mice?" grinned Detrick slyly.

Beth chimed in, setting the container in front of him. "These mice—the school property you promised to take care of, remember?"

"Just a minute, Beth," interrupted Mollie, facing Detrick head-on. "I'm not finished with him yet. Never mind the mice incident. Now you insult our friend, Yoshi. Just what are you trying to prove, Detrick Silver?"

Running his large hands through his long tousled hair, he smirked, picked up the container of mice, and casually walked out of the barn. On his way past Yoshi, he stuck out his foot, then laughed in Yoshi's face. Turning back to look at Mollie, he asked, "What's your problem? Do you *like* Slant Eyes?"

"Yoshi's a boy, just like you, Detrick. Only he has something you don't have—manners!" yelled Mollie.

She had hoped that Mr. Silver would notice the scuffle and discipline his son. But he was still engaged in deep conversation with Jess and Rose.

Yoshi seemed oblivious to the whole argument. Mollie was relieved that the language barrier had protected Yoshi from being hurt by Detrick's comments. Yoshi was still interested in watching the foal's every move.

"Did you hear him, Rose?" boiled Mollie, later. "He insulted Yoshi, and he doesn't care about anybody or anything but himself."

"I hate to bring up school during summer vacation, but this is what Miss Plerkins was talking about all last semester," said Caitlyn.

"Yeah, there's a word for it, and it's prejudice," said Mollie. "Prejudice is the most ignorant thing I ever heard of."

Beth reminded them, "Miss Plerkins said we students can make a difference in our world by fighting the effects of prejudice."

Sometimes Beth could be so factual that it was unnerving to Mollie. "Beth, how can we make a difference in our world when we can't even get through to one dumb football player named Detrick?"

Rose shook her head. "Whoa, girls, who says football players are dumb?"

Beth smiled. "Yes, Mollie, it's a prejudicial statement to say that football players are dumb."

"What?" said Mollie, growing louder and more defensive. "I didn't mean it that way."

Rose put her arm around Mollie's shoulders. "Relax, kiddo, I was just pointing out that sometimes we all say things that can hurt and divide people. Don't you think that Detrick has feelings too?"

"Yes, but," sputtered Mollie, "his attitude is making it impossible to be nice or patient. He insulted Yoshi."

"And he's picking on Yoshi just because he's from another country," added Caitlyn.

"OK," said Rose. "What can we do to help Detrick accept Yoshi?"

"Maybe," reflected Beth, "maybe we should try to accept Detrick just as he is."

"You mean ornery and rough and mean-as-a-snake Detrick?" said Mollie. "You're

51

kidding! Because that boy pulled a mouse prank, Savanna left the party early and probably will never come back again, if I know her."

"All is not lost, I'm sure," said Rose. "Come on in the house, girls, and let's cook Yoshi a pancake breakfast fit for a king. By the end of the summer, he won't ever want to go home to Tokyo."

Rose is something else, thought Mollie. Rose's heart was as big as all outdoors. Only a Christian like Rose could have compassion for Yoshi and Detrick at the same time. Suddenly, Mollie was sorry that she had blown up about Detrick. But she had never felt so mixed up in her life.

Could it be true that Mollie also had prejudice in her heart? She didn't think so, but then again, maybe she needed to pray about the matter. She was so confused that she decided not to think about it for a while. She would just enjoy the steaming, buttery stack of pancakes and maple syrup at Rose's inviting breakfast table.

All Mollie wanted was for life to be simple and carefree for her and her friends this summer. But judging from the way the first day had gone, she wasn't so sure "simple" and "carefree" was an accurate description . . .

10

Mollie's Prejudice

Even though she was thrilled about the new foal, Mollie went home after breakfast dragging her feet and sagging her shoulders. For someone who loved getting along with people so much, she wasn't being very successful at it, being at odds with Detrick and Savanna. She was sure her attitude had given Rose a poor impression!

She sat on the front steps and patted her cocker spaniel, Farley, for a while. Then she dragged herself into the house and up the stairs toward her room. She hoped not to meet anyone on the way, but it wasn't to be.

Her gloomy mood wasn't helped when Eric teased her about "smelling like a barn."

Then Charity bossed her about picking up her shoes and sweater she had dropped on the hall floor. Sometimes being the youngest in the family was the pits.

Just before slamming the door to her room, Mollie yelled, "You guys are just prejudiced against little sisters who love horses!"

Bang! Somehow slamming a door made Mollie feel better, then more miserable.

She could hear Mom asking Charity what the problem was. "I just asked Mollie to pick up the things she dropped in the hall. What's bugging her, Mom?"

Very softly, Mom tapped on the door of Mollie's room. Mollie sighed and asked her to come in.

"Want to talk about it?" asked Mom.

"No . . . yes . . . oh, Mom, I don't know what I want," Mollie's voice shook. Even though she wanted to be alone, she knew her mother still had that special way of easing into her heart and making things seem better. She could never hide things from Mom for very long.

Out came the whole story, about Yoshi staying with the Potters for the summer, that

Mollie wanted to help Yoshi have a great time while he was here; about Savanna leaving early because of Detrick Silver's prank with the mice in the barn; about Magic, the adorable new foal; about Detrick's prejudice against Yoshi; and now the worst part, about the possibility that Mollie could be prejudiced, too.

"You? Prejudiced?" asked Mom, surprised. "Why, you can strike up a conversation with anyone, even with the man in the moon. You never met a stranger, Mollie, and you always find something nice about everyone you meet."

"Not Detrick Silver," admitted Mollie. "I can't find anything nice about him, except that maybe he's a pretty good football player. But I don't even like football that much. I wish he wouldn't pick on Yoshi. Yoshi's so polite, Mom. He wouldn't hurt anyone. And that mean old rat, Detrick Silver, is treating him just awful."

"Mollie, please don't talk about others that way." Mother's voice got very serious. "We need to love others as Christ loves us."

"I'm sorry, Mom. I don't feel very loving right now," said Mollie, disappointed in herself.

Mom stroked Mollie's tangled hair and suggested that a shower would make her feel better. The warm water did soothe her tattered feelings.

When Mollie finished her shower, she could hear her mother talking softly on the phone. The only part of the conversation Mollie could hear was, "OK, I'll tell her. Thanks, Rose, for being there for Mollie these days. I'll be praying."

Mollie buttoned her top and wound her sopping wet hair into a towel turban as she scampered down the stairs. "Praying for what, Mom?"

"Were you eavesdropping?" Mom teased. Then she looked squarely into Mollie's hazel eyes. "Rose has called a special choir practice at her house this evening. She has talked with the pastor, who wants the youth to sing in the worship service Sunday. So you'll need to be at Rose's about 6:30."

Mollie could tell her mother knew more than she was saying. She also knew there was no sense trying to pry any remaining news out of her. She would just have to wait until tonight.

As usual, Mollie left a little earlier than necessary so that she could visit the horses for a while. Yoshi kept her company in the barn.

While they visited with Red and her foal, she and Yoshi practiced saying, "What's up, Buddy?" so that he could greet the other kids in a creative way. Yoshi taught Mollie to say, "Smile, be happy" in Japanese.

Perhaps Yoshi could tell that Mollie needed a friend, whether they could understand each other clearly or not. She couldn't help but smile.

The big farm bell sounded near the grape arbor. Yoshi and Mollie emerged from the barn and raced toward the grape arbor where other young people were gathering around Rose.

Savanna was there, sporting a new outfit, and looking around once in a while as if she might expect to see a mouse jump out at any time. Caitlyn was whispering and giggling with Savanna.

Beth sat down with Mollie and Yoshi under the arbor in the grass. Mollie noticed that the tractor was pulling into the barn. Soon, Detrick and Mr. Silver emerged, looking tired and dirty from their day in the fields.

Detrick walked past Yoshi, Mollie, and Beth and took a glass of lemonade from Rose.

"Is Slant Eyes still here?" muttered Detrick under his breath.

Before Mollie could respond, Rose invited Detrick to stay for choir practice. Mollie stared at Rose in disbelief! Whatever possessed Rose to do that? She held her breath, waiting for Detrick to say "no," which he most certainly would. But for a long moment, he just stood there in his sweaty, dirty T-shirt and jeans, wiped his brow, and grinned uncertainly.

Finally, he said, "Sure, Mrs. Potter, I'll stay."

"Good deal!" exclaimed Rose while Beth and Mollie exchanged blank looks. "Come up here and sit in front beside Eric and David."

In Rose's typical animated style, she got the whole group involved in a warm-up praise song. Only Detrick didn't sing. He spent most of the time looking over his shoulder at Yoshi and smirking as if to make fun at Yoshi's efforts to mouth the American words.

"Hold me back," Mollie whispered to Beth between songs. "I feel the urge to just haul off and punch Detrick right in the nose. Yoshi is a nice, decent boy from another country. Detrick is a tough guy who doesn't know how to act. What's his problem anyway?"

"Mollie . . . ," interrupted Beth.

Mollie continued to fume until she realized Rose was standing right behind her. She felt Rose's gentle but firm touch on the back of her shoulder. Suddenly, Mollie was terribly ashamed. She was sorry that Rose, who seemed to like everyone, had caught her in another moment of frustration.

11

A Mixed-Up Heart

Rose kept her cheerful composure and got the group on their feet to do a few praise songs with motions. By the time they had gone into a round of "I've Got a River of Life Flowing Out of Me," everyone was really revved up about singing as a choir.

"OK, sit down and get comfortable, everybody. Let's learn a new song for Sunday morning. It's about Jesus' love for all people. I believe it has a great message for each of us. Here's how it goes," Rose began to sing with the cassette tape accompaniment.

The song had to do with Jesus holding out His hands to all the people of the world, including the rich, the poor, the sick, and the hurting—everyone. While the song appealed to Mollie, she couldn't bring herself to sing with the others. Her heart felt as gray as the little heart mark on Magic's nose.

She was beginning to realize a terrible truth, that she really was prejudiced against Detrick Silver. She had been blind to the fact that God did make him and loves him, though Mollie wasn't quite sure why.

She knew she had to work through her anger and somehow forgive Detrick, but how? Mollie turned to glance at Detrick. To her surprise, he was gone!

Only Beth noticed when Mollie slipped out of the grape arbor. She felt that she might suffocate if she remained there with everyone. She just wanted to be with Red and Magic.

As she walked to the barn, she mulled over her confused thoughts. Mollie didn't like the idea of being prejudiced against someone, even when it was someone like Detrick.

"Dear God," she whispered, "please forgive me and help my heart to change toward Detrick. And please help Detrick, too. And protect Yoshi from feeling unloved. . . .

At the barn entrance Mollie felt

something even before she heard it. Glancing around, she saw Detrick offering an apple to Red. They both gasped with surprise.

"Uh, uh . . . ," Detrick said, looking down. "Uh, I just wanted to check on Red and Magic."

He turned and hurried out into the evening shadows. In the quiet of the barn, with only the consoling noises that the horses made when they talked to each other, Mollie tried to sort out her feelings. *What could have made Detrick come to the barn? Just this morning he put her down for being so excited about Magic.*

After choir practice ended, Rose, Savanna, Caitlyn, and Beth came running into the barn out of breath. "We've been looking for you everywhere," gasped Caitlyn.

Mollie smiled. "Didn't you know I'd be here of all places with little Magic and Red?"

"Duh," said Caitlyn, pretending to knock her head hard against her hand.

"Are you OK, Mollie?" asked Savanna. She had a sincere look of concern on her face.

"Sure," said Mollie. "I'm just a little ashamed of myself, and I don't know what to do about it."

She looked pleadingly at Rose. "Can you ever forgive me for my bad attitude toward Detrick? I didn't like the way he was treating Yoshi. I guess maybe I haven't given Detrick a chance. But he sure can be a bully sometimes."

Savanna chimed in, "Yes, he even scuffed up my aerobic shoes on purpose the last day of school. Can you believe it?"

Then Caitlyn volunteered, "That's nothing. He smells and doesn't care how he acts or what people think about him."

"That's where you're probably very wrong," said Rose.

The girls grew quiet. Rose continued, "I think Detrick cares very much what you think of him, and I believe he tries harder than you think he does."

"Could you explain that, Rose?" asked Beth. Even brainy Beth couldn't figure this one out.

"Girls, you need to be careful not to share what I'm about to tell you. But I think it will help you understand Detrick better," said Rose in a low, serious voice. "You see, Detrick was adopted just recently."

"Adopted? You mean the Silvers aren't

Detrick's real parents?" asked Mollie.

"That's right," said Rose. "His mother died, and he was abused by his father. He was in and out of foster homes until last year, when he came to live with the Silvers. They adopted him and moved away from the city. They're trying to help him deal with the many problems that his past created for him."

Mollie closed her eyes. Poor Detrick! She couldn't imagine a father who abused his child, because her dad was the kindest, most decent man she knew.

Rose took a deep breath. "Girls, it's hard for Detrick to trust other people. He was in so many different homes with so many different kinds of people, that he hasn't known who to believe or trust. He was taught some wrong things along the way, including how to treat people a different color from himself."

Savanna looked down at her shoes. "So that's why he called me names at school a lot."

Mollie was surprised. "You never told us that he called you names, Savanna."

"My chocolate skin makes me different, you know," she said sadly. "I guess that's why he has given Yoshi a bad time of it."

Rose shook her head. "Many adults have the wrong ideas about people. That's why through American history there have been times marked by slavery and prejudice of all kinds. Some adults pass these ridiculous ideas along to children."

"I have to tell you something," said Caitlyn, breaking the silence. She began to admit that when she was younger she thought all Japanese people were bad because her grandfather had been killed by a Japanese air fighter pilot during World War II.

"At first, I wasn't really excited about getting to know Yoshi," she said slowly, "but when I found out he could play baseball, I decided it was silly to hold a grudge against a boy who didn't have a thing to do with a war such a long time ago."

Mollie's heart, which had felt all twisted and angry, began to melt with compassion. "I never knew that about you, Caitlyn. I thought we had told each other everything. It must be terrible not to have known your grandfather."

"But more terrible to hate a whole set of people just because I couldn't meet him," said Caitlyn sadly. "I know I'll see my granddad in

66

heaven someday. I'm sure we'll play baseball and eat hot dogs with chili together for years at a time."

Rose patted Caitlyn's hand. Beth, who had been listening thoughtfully, suddenly spoke up. "How did Detrick come to be adopted by the Silvers?"

"It's a long story," said Rose, "but Mr. Silver was a street kid in the inner city when he was small. A Christian farm family took him in at an early age, and he wanted to do the same for another boy when he was able to support a son. Detrick came to live with the Silvers last year just before they bought the farm and moved here."

Mollie sighed. "This really does help me understand better. But has everyone forgotten how ornery Detrick is? Just because he had a rough home life doesn't mean that the way he treats people is right."

"True," said Rose. "But remember he has to be shown how to love, how to trust. That's why we must endure his tough-guy attitude. That attitude helped him survive and cope under difficult circumstances. He will learn to trust, but it will take time."

Mollie was amazed by Rose's understanding of kids. Rose lifted Mollie's chin until their eyes met. "We need to be patient with people like Detrick. He's in a good Christian home now. We want to show the love of Jesus to him, dear Miss Mollie."

Now she finally understood how truly wrong she had been in her attitude toward Detrick. Still, she was concerned for Yoshi in a country that's strange to him. How could she be a friend to both boys? They were worlds apart in their behavior. Jesus! He would help her find a way.

"I guess I need to say something too," said Beth, looking embarrassed. She turned to Savanna. "I've often judged people who were concerned with their looks and had all the latest clothes. I'm sorry, Savanna. I think you are one of the nicest girls in school. God made you pretty, and I'm really glad you're my friend."

Savanna burst into laughter. "Guess what? I always thought you were such a bookworm that you never noticed whether your socks matched. Well, I like you just as you are because our friendship is a perfect match!"

Jumping up and down, Mollie declared,

"Do you know what this means? We're all really, really friends again! It happened! For all of our differences, we are closer than ever. And Jesus is the glue that sticks us together!"

"Vive le difference!" shouted Savanna.

"Here, here," agreed Beth.

"Whatever," said Caitlyn, giggling.

"Let's pray!" suggested Rose.

The girls huddled with Rose for the best prayer meeting Mollie had ever experienced. They thanked God for each other, for the special qualities that made each girl unique, for Yoshi, and yes, for Detrick. Mollie freely admitted her mistake to God and asked Him to give her a chance to be glue that could bring together those two boys from opposite sides of the globe.

The summer was suddenly looking up . . .

12

Mollie's Decision

As the girls and Rose hugged each other, Mollie felt a something tugging at her ponytail. "Hey!" she exclaimed and turned around to discover Magic"s nose protruding through the stall fencing.

"Little girl, I need my hair, if you don't mind," she said, rubbing Magic's nose, where the little heart birthmark had appeared. The newborn filly whinnied and nuzzled her hand, then turned and ran across the stall playfully.

"She likes you, Mollie," said Savanna. "Say, I think I might be starting to like horses, too—at least baby ones!"

Wide-eyed, Mollie stared at Savanna and smiled a smile as big as the moon that was rising in the evening sky. "Wow, now that's a miracle!"

The other girls laughed heartily. Only Rose seemed deep in thought. "Ladies, I think I have a plan. Come on!"

Even though it was 8 P.M. already and most adults were thinking of settling in for the night, Rose was just getting started. Pretty soon, Mollie and her friends were elbow-deep in flour and eggs and milk and brown sugar. Two large coffee cakes were in the works.

At last, they came out of the oven. By then the girls and Yoshi were longing for a warm slice with milk. Noticing that half a coffee cake and two quarts of milk were disappearing, Rose and Jess announced that the girls might as well sleep over.

"We keep extra sleeping bags in the barn just for times like this, Rose said. "Then in the morning we'll take the other coffee cake to Detrick and his family." Her voice trailed off at the end of her sentence. She seemed to be waiting for Mollie's reaction.

But Mollie just smiled. She knew what Rose was up to. She knew the coffee cake was a peace offering, an act of friendship. But she

71

wondered, Will Detrick accept our friendship? If he does, it will definitely be a miracle.

This time, with her parents' permission, Savanna joined Caitlyn, Beth, and Mollie in the barn. She actually seemed pretty comfortable nestling into a sleeping bag on a hard tackroom floor. She didn't complain about the dust, or her new jeans getting messy. She even tried not to sneeze from breathing hay. When the girls heard something rustle in the darkness, Savanna squealed a little. But Mollie thought all in all, Savanna was really being brave!

The nicest part was that the girls were like pieces of a puzzle, fitting together nicely to make a whole. Here they were, each so different, celebrating friendship into the wee hours of the night. Soft laughter and stars and the gentle touch of a newborn foal blended together to create the greatest fun Mollie could ever remember having.

Caitlyn, Savanna, and Beth were still snoozing soundly the next morning when Mollie heard the barn door swing open, then close gently. Her bones felt a little stiff in the cool morning air. She could have easily rolled over herself and gone back to sleep deep in the fleeced lining of the sleeping bag.

But the sound of footsteps and a low, "Whoa, Filly" told Mollie that Jess was out early for the morning feeding. Yawning deeply, she wandered out to help.

"Hello, Mollie Jane," he called, as she leaned over to stroke Mittye Kitty, who was nibbling at her cat food. Then he added, "What's got you looking so serious this morning?"

"Jess," she began, "have you ever been prejudiced about something or someone?"

Jess looked surprised at such a question. He thought for a long time before he answered. "You are jumping into the deep end with a question like that, little girl."

While Mollie might have protested being called "little girl" by anyone else, it was a high compliment coming from Jess. They were buddies.

"Yes," Jess reflected, "I suppose that on occasion I have realized that an opinion I had was hurtful to someone. I guess that's prejudice all right."

"What did you do to make it right?" asked Mollie. She helped Jess separate a bale of hay

73

into two flakes for each horse as he pondered her second question.

"You're going to use up all my words for the day with questions like these," Jess said, chuckling a little uncertainly. "Well, seems to me one time when I was about 10 years old, my parents hired a few migrant workers to help during the harvest. Their children and I would play for hours in the barn, in the trees, and we'd sneak up to old man Whitaker's place for some apples out of his orchard. Don't hold that against me now," he added.

"I won't," Mollie said, with a smile. That's what she liked most about Jess. He didn't pretend to be all perfect, so it was easy for Mollie to be herself with him. "What happened?"

"Oh, we had a good time until some of my pals from school stopped by and made fun of the migrant workers and their youngsters. They asked me why I would play with such scruffy-looking, dark-skinned kids.

"I guess I was worried about what my friends from school thought about me, and I decided not to play with my new friends anymore. I know I must have hurt their feelings pretty bad," Jess said regretfully.

"Then what?" asked Mollie.

"That's it," said Jess, shaking his head a little sadly. "If I could go back, I'd have gone right on playing with those migrant workers' children. But they moved on to another place, and I never got to say 'I'm sorry.' I still think about those kids now and then and wonder where they are."

Then Jess looked deep into Mollie's eyes. "Don't let that happen to you, Mollie Jane. Always be fair with people, and you'll grow up without regrets."

Mollie smiled. Her heart thumped a little wildly, thinking about going to the Silvers' home this morning. But she knew that she had to do it. In fact, now she wanted to do it.

"Thanks, Jess," she whispered.

13

Mollie's Miracle

Jess and Mollie decided to play a joke on the other girls, so they got some old chains hanging in the tack room and clanked them together. Caitlyn and Savanna jumped sky-high, but Beth slept through the whole thing.

"Come on, Sleeping Beauty," said Caitlyn. "If I can't sleep, you can't sleep, either."

"*Ohhh*," groaned Beth. "Can't a future vet get some shut-eye?"

Mollie shook Beth vigorously. "Come on, we're going to the Silvers' today."

Beth opened one eye. "Mollie, you actually sound almost happy about that."

"Let's just say I'm hopeful," Mollie replied.

Rose wouldn't let them go until they had all had a shower after the chores were done. Scrubbed clean, they finally hopped into Jess's truck. Beth was assigned to hold the coffee cake they had baked for the Silvers because Rose figured she was least likely to nibble it on the way.

Rose started the engine, backed up a few feet, then stepped on the brake. Alarmed, she said, "We forgot Yoshi!"

Just then, Yoshi ran out the back door with a big bag and climbed into the truck next to Mollie. "Wait for Yoshi," he said with a grin. Laughing and singing, they made the winding trek to the Silvers' farm.

Just as they were turning into the driveway, Mollie felt a little sick. "OK, God," she prayed silently. "It's all up to You. I can't do this without You."

"Maybe they won't be home," said Savanna. It was obvious that she was just as nervous about this visit as Mollie was.

But there was Detrick, playing basketball in the driveway. He continued to shoot hoops as Rose parked the truck.

As if frozen in time, the girls just sat there

while Yoshi scrambled out with his bag. "Just be yourselves," said Rose, "and let God take care of the rest."

"Here goes nothing," said Mollie, gulping hard.

But much to their surprise and delight, Detrick smiled ever so slightly and invited them into the house. He continued to play basketball, so the girls and Yoshi followed Rose through the back door into the family room.

Mrs. Silver was hanging up the telephone, as they greeted her. Like her name, her hair sparkled with whitish silver streaks, and her eyes glimmered pleasantly. "Well, it's nice to see the neighbors! Please, everyone, won't you sit down? Can I get you something to wet your whistle?"

Yoshi looked confused. "Wet whistle?"

Mollie grinned. "Drink, Yoshi. Are you thirsty?" She motioned with her hand as though she were taking a drink.

"Ah," said Yoshi, with a bow, "whistle plenty wet, thank you."

Rose introduced Yoshi and each of the girls to Mrs. Silver. Mollie remembered that she met Mr. and Mrs. Silver at church once after the Easter cantata.

"Land sakes, how Mollie has grown!" exclaimed Mrs. Silver. "And Yoshi, how nice to have you visit us in Tennessee."

Yoshi bowed politely, even though Mollie was pretty sure he couldn't understand all the words.

"You have a very cozy home, Mrs. Silver," said Caitlyn.

Mollie was thinking the same thing. It wasn't fancy, but it was warm and inviting, and it smelled like French vanilla. One could tell by a glance that Mrs. Silver had a knack for making crafts, which dotted the walls and bookshelves with color and creativity. A framed photograph of Detrick with Mr. and Mrs. Silver rested on the coffee table.

"Did you see Detrick on your way in?" Mrs. Silver asked. The girls nodded politely. "He's working so hard in the fields these days, I told him to take the morning off and just enjoy the sunshine."

Mollie and Savanna exchanged glances. How amazing Mrs. Silver's kindness was toward such a hard character like Detrick! She had to be some sort of angel. But Mollie was glad that

Detrick had a good set of parents now.

"That's why we came this morning," said Rose, "to brag on your son and your husband for doing such fine work in our fields yesterday. Here are the checks Jess sent along, and the girls brought something for your family, too."

Beth presented the coffee cake to Mrs. Silver. "What a surprise!" she exclaimed, throwing up her hands. "Thank you, young ladies. Won't you help us eat it?"

All the girls laughed. "We've been eating coffee cake since last night," said Caitlyn. "First, we devoured half of one last night, and then we ate the other half this morning for breakfast. We couldn't eat another bite, believe me!"

Detrick came in. "Ma, what smells so good?" he asked, sniffing around the coffee cake.

Mollie couldn't help but grin. Pretty soon, Detrick was gobbling up a man-sized helping with an open container of milk straight out of the refrigerator.

"Detrick, what do you say to the girls?" coaxed Mrs. Silver.

Detrick looked up, puzzled for a moment.

"Oh, uh, thanks. It's good."

"You're welcome," said Rose cheerfully.

Yoshi had surprises, too. As he opened a bag and began pulling out a gift for Mrs. Silver and one for Detrick, Rose explained the lovely Japanese custom of bringing gifts to hosts and friends in America.

Mrs. Silver opened her carefully wrapped gift. "What lovely notepaper! How delicate and fine! Thank you, Yoshi!"

Yoshi gave Detrick his gift. Mollie held her breath. Would Detrick accept it and be nice?

Detrick shook his head. "I don't want a present," he said.

Mrs. Silver encouraged him. "Detrick, he wants you to have it. Go ahead now."

Scratching his head, Detrick grinned uncomfortably. "Thanks."

But when he opened it, Mollie saw the delight in his eyes. Inside the box were materials for making a brightly colored paper kite.

Mrs. Silver suggested that Detrick take Yoshi and the girls outdoors. They could assemble the kite on the picnic table in the garden and then try out the kite. Mollie looked at

Rose wistfully, hoping that she would be rescued. But Rose agreed wholeheartedly.

"Coming with us, Rose?" asked Mollie.

"I'll just sit here and chat with Mrs. Silver," she said, urging Mollie out the door with her eyes.

"Show them a good time, now, Detrick," called Mrs. Silver, as they made their way out the sliding glass door.

They stepped into an English garden with all kinds of summer flowers in full bloom at bird feeders hanging or fastened from every possible tree limb and post. Mollie's eyes were bathed in color and the wonderful fragrance tickled her nose.

"This is beautiful!" exclaimed Caitlyn. "Look at this little bridge over the creek!"

"Yeah, my dad and I built that," said Detrick.

"Wow," said Mollie, "you have a lot of talent."

Detrick looked surprised. He shrugged his shoulders, but a faint smile crept across his face.

Savanna pointed to a large yellow blossom. "That flower reminds me of one that grew in our yard in Jamaica."

"You're from Jamaica? Where's that?" asked Detrick.

"Below the United States, in the Caribbean," said Savanna. "It's very warm and sunny there. I was born in Jamaica."

"Oh," said Detrick, studying the dirt on his shoes. "I was born in Chicago, but I don't remember much." Then he gestured at Yoshi. "Where was he born?"

"Tokyo," said Mollie, "in Japan."

"Oh," said Detrick.

"By the way," began Beth, "how are the mice doing?"

Mollie was starting to wish Beth hadn't brought up that subject, when Detrick said, "Fine. Hey, uh, I'm sorry about the other night. It won't happen again."

Then Caitlyn chirped, "That's OK, we found out they like Yoshi's dried squid snacks from Japan." Then, it happened. Detrick actually laughed.

Before they knew it, they had the kite put together. For the rest of the morning, they took turns flying it through the Silvers' meadow, and Yoshi demonstrated some kite-flying techniques that kept it doing loop-the-loop tricks non-stop.

83

Here they were—Caitlyn, Beth, Savanna, Yoshi, Detrick, and Mollie, flying a kite together like old pals. And they were actually having a pretty good time! This was the miracle Mollie had prayed for, only God was working it out much better than she could have hoped.

As they were piling into the truck to leave, Rose asked Detrick to come sing with the youth group on Sunday at church. "Thanks, but that's OK," said Detrick, glancing at his mom.

After a lot of argument, Detrick said he would "think about it." Then he tapped Yoshi on the back. "Thanks for the kite, man."

Mollie paused before she boarded the truck. Looking back at Detrick, she said, "Everything would be perfect, if you'd say you'll sing with us tomorrow. Besides, it's my birthday, and that's what I wish for." And she really meant it.

14

Happy Birthday Again, Mollie

That Sunday, Mollie awoke feeling much older and wiser. Yes, she felt 12 all over! The first thing she did was pray that Detrick would be in the youth choir this morning.

About halfway through Sunday School, in walked Detrick and Yoshi together! Rose was smiling in the doorway at Mollie's astonished expression, as they took their seats.

After class Mollie found Rose and asked, "How did you get those two together?"

"Actually, they're getting to be quite good buddies," Rose replied. "Come to the farm after lunch today, if you can."

"OK! You don't have to ask me twice," said Mollie.

Later that morning as they sang in the choir for the worship service, Mollie couldn't decide who was singing louder—Detrick or Yoshi! "Spread Jesus' love and kindness to everyone," rang the lyrics all the way from Mollie's toes. This time as Mollie sang the words, joy filled her heart, until she was sure that she would spill over on Savanna next to her.

As the number concluded, many parents and friends in the congregation smiled or nodded in approval. But Jess seemed to be the proudest of all.

Rose winked at the choir as she seated them. That meant "Wow—great job" in sign language, Rose-style.

Mollie wasn't sure what the sermon was about, because she silently pondered how Jesus had broken down real walls of prejudice between Yoshi and Detrick. Most of all, she thanked Him for destroying the prejudice in her own heart.

As a result, she had an unlikely new friend, Detrick Silver. In addition, she felt so much closer to Savanna, Caitlyn, Beth, Rose, and Jess than ever before.

It surprised Mollie that her whole family wanted to accompany her to Jess and Rose's that afternoon. Eric simply despised horses, and Charity was always complaining that Mollie spent too much time talking about them. So they usually avoided going to the Potters' farm like a bad toothache.

This time, though, there was a race to the car. "Hurry up, Mollie," called out her dad. "I want to get back in time to take my Sunday afternoon nap."

When they drove up, the Potters didn't seem to be home. The truck was nowhere in sight. Mollie put her hands on her hips. "Now why did Rose ask me to come over here if she isn't at home?"

Mom had a funny look in her eyes. "Well, we can go home and come back later. But before we go, why don't you check in the barn, just in case?"

"You don't have to ask me twice," Mollie said her favorite line. She dashed to the barn to see the horses.

When she opened the barn door, there stood Yoshi, holding a lead rope. On the other end of the rope was little Magic, with a large red bow attached to her baby halter.

"Happy Birthday, Mollie," said Yoshi with a bow.

One by one, people began to step out of nowhere and everywhere, from all points in the barn. There were Beth and one of her sisters, Caitlyn, Caitlyn's mom, Savanna and her parents, Detrick, Mr. and Mrs. Silver, Mom, Dad, Eric, Charity, Jess, and Rose.

"What's going on?" asked Mollie. Even as she asked the question, she was hoping, just hoping that she knew the answer.

Rose and Jess joined Mollie in the middle of the barn. Yoshi brought Magic closer. The foal's perfectly pointed ears seeming to soak up every word, as though she could understand.

"Mollie," said Rose, "your mom and dad agree with Jess and me that you have made some great choices and demonstrated a lot of kindness toward others. We all believe that you are mature enough to take on more chores and more responsibility."

Mollie's mom's eyes were misting up, while Dad shot a video. "Mollie," he said, "that little bit of Magic you see in front of you is yours now. We've worked it out so that she can board right here at the Potters', but you'll have to take care of her and teach her how to be a Tennessee walking horse."

For a moment, Mollie couldn't breathe. Could it be possible that this was really happening? Finally, she found her voice as she hugged her very own, perfectly beautiful, brand-new foal.

"This is the most wonderful gift I could ever receive . . ." Then she looked around her and added, "besides friends."

About the Author

Renée Holmes Kent is a freelance writer and desktop publisher. She owns a small business called Promotional Expressions. She and Mel Kent have been married for 21 years and have three children, Matt, Melissa, and Mary-Alison. They live in West Liberty, Ohio.

Can you tell that Renée shares Mollie's love of Tennessee walking horses? She and her youngest daughter Mary-Alison spend their spare time at the farm of Gary and Jude Rose, owners of the 1996 World Grand Champion, Lightfoot's Wildfire. They love riding Hershey (Mary-Alison's pony), grooming horses, and working with foals (especially Phoebe).

Renée is a University of Tennessee graduate (Communications). She is a loyal Big Orange football and basketball fan and misses her walks in the Smoky Mountains. In Ohio, Renée travels the Buckeye state helping establish Women on Mission groups in Baptist churches. She wrote *Kelli's Discovery, Yes You Can, Kelli!* and *You Can Be a Musician and a Missionary, Too.*